Claiming Valentine

The Claiming Series
Book 7

Violet Rae

Author's Note

Thank you for choosing to read Claiming Valentine. This book features a main character with Asperger's Syndrome.

Asperger's Syndrome is a form of Autism Spectrum Syndrome, a neurobiological disorder where people have difficulty relating to others socially. Their behavior and thinking patterns can be rigid and repetitive.

Raising awareness of autism is a cause close to my heart as my son is on the autistic spectrum. Each person experiences autism differently, but it's important to know that it's not a "disease," and it's not something that needs to be "cured," but rather needs to be understood and embraced.

Claiming Valentine is a work of fiction and aims to highlight some of the struggles people face on the spectrum through Tasha and Link's love story.

Thank you to my friends in the author community (you know who you are) whom I value greatly.

And to you, my readers, I truly hope you enjoy this story. Thank you from the bottom of my heart for all the support you have shown me over the last year.

Happy reading,

Violet

Blurb

He sees her heart, not her challenges—now he'll do anything to prove they're meant to be.

Link

I visit Valentine's Kitchen every day, trying to work up the courage to ask Natasha Valentine on a date. Delicious as her bakery's treats are, they don't compare to her sweet curves, ebony hair, and deep-brown eyes. I'm hooked from the first day.

When our first date ends disastrously, I'm left wondering where I went wrong. Walking away from her isn't an option because Tasha is unlike any woman I've ever known. I'm drawn to her in ways that go deeper than physical attraction.

Tasha thinks her Asperger's is a problem to keep us apart. I see it as a gift, an opportunity to connect, communicate, and understand each other better than many couples have the chance to do. I'll do whatever it takes to be the man she deserves, and earn my place at her side for the rest of our lives.

Chapter 1
Tasha

Mornings are my favorite time of the day. It's just me in the kitchen with all my ingredients. I make sure to get them ready the night before, so all I need to do is take them out and put them in the order I'm going to use them.

I unlock the door of Valentine's Kitchen at 4 AM, as I do every morning except Sundays. It's not like I have far to go, living in the apartment above the bakery. The sun isn't even up yet, and the streets are so peaceful. There are no people around, which suits me fine—I'll have plenty of customers to deal with later once the doors open.

I inhale deeply as I enter the shop. The kitchen still smells delicious from all the baked goods yesterday, and the aroma is comforting. I slip automatically into my morning routine, starting with preparing my coffee. I have a special brew I like to make up just for me. The beans are in the fridge, and I enjoy the sound of them grinding. The smell they release is pure heaven.

I can't tolerate many sounds and smells, but the sound and smell of grinding coffee beans isn't one of them.

While the coffee brews, I get my kitchen set up how I like it.

I know I could come in later and still finish all my work for the day. I wouldn't have to go to bed so early. But being alone in my kitchen, doing things my way, and not worrying about someone moving something when I'm not looking is my idea of heaven.

By the time the coffee is done brewing and my counter-tops are set up with all the ingredients I plan to use for baking, the sun is starting to come up.

I like that there aren't any cars on the streets yet. The only sound is the birds waking up. I stand at the back door, letting the cool breeze caress my skin as I talk to the birds.

"Good morning, tweeters," I croon, watching them swoop and land, wings twitching and heads bobbing as they peck at the cake crumbs I've tossed on the ground

I've called birds tweeters ever since I was a child. My mom likes to tell the story about how I would kneel on the couch at the window, chattering in my baby talk. The only thing she could understand was the word "tweeters." I'm not sure where I came up with that. Even now, as an adult, I can't seem to make the switch to calling them birds, like every other adult on the face of the earth. I've stopped trying. So long as *I* know what I mean, does it matter?

"I'm making some jam tarts today and, of course, fresh bread. What are you doing? Building nests? I'll bring you some more treats later."

It's never occurred to me that talking to birds might be strange. On some level, I know people might think so, but I'm beyond the point of trying to be "normal"— whatever that means. Just more boxes to tick and try to fit into.

I head back inside just as Alexa, my regular day staff, arrives. I'm fortunate I don't need more than one employee at a time because I can't deal with too many people around me.

Alexa opens up the bakery for the day and serves the customers out front while I immerse myself in my baking out back in the kitchen.

As I work, my focus is interrupted for the briefest moment. A masculine face slides into my mind, and I shake my head to get rid of it. I don't like being interrupted when I'm baking—even if it is my own random thoughts about a certain handsome guy with bright blue eyes who comes in every day.

"Tasha, can I leave early today?" Alexa asks, appearing

behind me a couple of hours later as I mix up the batter for the muffins.

At eighteen, Alexa is unpredictable and impulsive at times. Although, I shouldn't blame her age. Unpredictability and impulsiveness are foreign concepts to me. My life is one of structure and routine.

The idea of breaking our daily schedule makes me anxious. "Is it necessary?"

"I'm sorry, but yes, it is. I've had a horrible toothache for days, and I've been taking a shit ton, uh, I mean, a lot of painkillers, but they're not helping. The dentist just called to say there's a cancellation," Alexa explains with what I think is a pleading expression. "I said I'd take it. I need to be there by 2 PM."

I take a deep breath, reminding myself that this isn't a big deal. It's usually quiet after that time, and I can easily manage myself. I'll just need to cover on my own until 4 PM when Lisa comes in.

I nod my head. "I understand. Of course, you should go and take care of that."

"Thanks, Tasha," Alexa replies gratefully.

I nod. "No problem."

Alexa returns to the counter, and I take a break to call my best friend, Belle. She and I trained together at Molly Black's culinary school in Medicine Bow. Her training was interrupted by her mother's death, and her grandmother came to take her back to Jasper and the ranch where she grew up. I need to check in with her and find out how she's doing.

"Hey, Tash," Belle greets me after the second ring.

"How are you?" I ask immediately.

"Ah, you know." Belle sighs down the line. "Actually, you don't, do you?" she asks, although the question is rhetorical.

Belle gets me better than anyone other than my parents. She's never made me feel awkward and never treated me any differently.

"Let's see," she continues. "I've just lost my mom, Grams is dying of cancer, and a month ago, I married a man I've been in love with for years to protect the ranch and my inheritance. So, yeah, I guess overwhelmed is one way of putting it," she says dryly.

I know all about feeling overwhelmed, although mine is more of a physical stimuli thing. "I'm sorry. That sucks. Want me to package up some of my chocolate cupcakes and mail them to you?" I ask, coming up with the only way I know how to cheer her up.

"That would be amazing. You know how much I love your cupcakes. Almost as much as I love your pastries."

"Ah, my croissants and pain au chocolat. I'll make some just for you," I promise.

"What would I do without you?"

"Not have cupcakes, croissants, or pain au chocolat."

Belle's soft laugh reaches me down the line. "True. So how are things in Garland? Is Valentine's Kitchen still pulling in the customers?"

Belle and I talk for a few more minutes before I need to get back to work. It's always good to hear my friend's voice, and we promise to call again in a few days.

The next couple of hours fly, and before I know it, Alexa is heading out the door for her dental appointment. Just after she leaves, the door chime jingles, and I look up with my professional smile firmly fixed on my face.

It's *him*. Link Thompson.

Steely blue eyes, strong nose, high cheekbones, and a body that makes me weak in the knees. I hate it when he comes in and makes me feel this way. So out of control. But I love it at the same time.

"Good morning, Tasha."

His deep voice makes my heart jump around. I could listen to him talk all day. If only he wanted to talk to me for that long.

"Good morning, Link." I give him what I think passes for a genuine smile. "What can I get for you today?"

"Well, that depends," he says, blue eyes twinkling. "What are you offering?"

"I made some jam tarts this morning. There's raspberry, strawberry, and blueberry," I reply, pointing them out in the display case.

"Those sound good. I'm sure the guys at the garage will love them. Can I get half a dozen? Two of each?"

I busy myself with putting them in a box.

"And three cups of that amazing coffee you make."

"One black, the other two are cream and sugar, right?"

Link shakes his head and laughs.

I frown. Did I say something funny?

"You have the best memory of anyone I've ever met," he says, and I think that's appreciation I see in his eyes as he looks at me.

I'm not vain, but I know the opposite sex finds me physically attractive. I'm not beautiful, but my long, black hair and abundant curves seem to appeal to men—not that I've taken up the offer of a date with either of the men who've asked me since I moved here. They may like the packaging, but they have no idea how to deal with the woman beneath the pretty wrapping paper.

"I'm just good with details," I reply in response to Link's comment. "I know the black coffee is for you. I remember you telling me you don't like messing up your coffee with cream and sugar. And the other two are for Brett and Jim, who seem to have no problem destroying a perfectly good cup of coffee with both" I wrinkle my nose in distaste.

"I know, right?" Link agrees with a smile. "I keep threatening to set the coffee police on them."

I tilt my head as I look at him. "That's a real thing?"

Link's blond eyebrows rise. "The coffee police? No, but it should be," he replies with a wink that makes my stomach flutter.

I finish putting the coffees in a tray and hand them to him along with the box of pastries before giving him the total.

Carefully, Link counts out the exact change. He always has exact change. I appreciate that. Most people these days use debit cards, but Link always seems to have cash.

"Thank you, Link."

He lingers for a moment, and I wonder if he's forgotten something. Or maybe I did. What did I forget?

"Are you going to the fishing derby this weekend?" he asks.

I can't stop myself from making a face. "No, I don't fish."

He laughs. "No. You don't strike me as someone who fishes."

I wonder what that means, but I don't know how to ask. Everyone around here fishes, and they seem to think it's fun. I don't get it. I just feel bad for those poor fish. They get hooked and then thrown back into the lake like they're supposed to go about their lives after being teased by worms, only to end up on a hook. It must be so traumatic.

"What do you do for fun, Tasha?"

I wonder why he's asking me these questions, but I answer anyway. "I bake."

"That's your job. What do you do when you aren't baking?"

I don't understand the question. Baking is fun. "I, um, I eat what I bake. Or I sell it. Or sometimes, I take it to the shelter because I know they don't get sweet treats very often. I like watching people enjoy what I make."

He studies me thoughtfully. "That's generous of you. Do you eat stuff other than your baking?"

Such a silly question. "Of course."

"Would you like to eat stuff other than your baking with me sometime?" he asks.

Company would be nice. I think. I usually eat whatever is simple and easy at home with my cat, George.

I nod. "Sure."

"Great."

The smile on his face tells me I've given the right answer, and it sets off a spark inside me. I've made him happy. That makes me feel warm inside. It's not a feeling I'm overly familiar with.

"How about tonight?"

Tonight? I panic. My favorite show is on at 9 PM. That's later than my usual bedtime, but I come in a little later on Saturdays, so I can stay up until 10 PM. Will I be home in time to watch my show?

"I guess I could do that. I have to be home by nine, though. You know I live in the apartment above the bakery, right?" I ask, pointing a finger toward the ceiling.

He grins. "Oh, believe me, I know."

He reaches out and touches my hand, and I pull back instinctively. The unexpected tactile contact takes me by surprise, and the warmth of his skin does odd things to my heart rate.

Link frowns. "I'm sure I can have you home by then, but only if you're sure you want to go."

"I do," I say, reassuring him—and myself.

I *do* want to eat with Link. I don't think he considers this a date or anything, but it would be nice to have him as a friend.

Chapter 2
Link

I walk back to the garage with the coffee and tarts, mulling over my conversation with Tasha.

Natasha Valentine is a mystery to me.

Sometimes, I think she's attracted to me the way I'm attracted to her. Other times, like when she pulled her hand away, I think I'm totally off track.

From the day she re-opened the old bakery after the previous owner retired—aptly renaming it Valentine's Kitchen—I've been hooked on seeing her. I swear, I've gained ten pounds from all the pastry I've been eating. I promise myself I'll go to the gym for a quick workout after work if I can get off a little early today.

Tasha is unlike any other woman I've ever met. She doesn't throw herself at me. Quite the opposite. She's withdrawn and quiet, and sometimes, she looks like she's lost in her own little world.

Maybe I'm chasing rainbows, thinking I stand a chance with someone as beautiful as her.

Maybe I'm just another customer as far as she's concerned.

But she's way more than that to me. I've been trying to figure out a way to ask her out for weeks. I've danced around it by asking things like whether she was going to the charity dance at the town hall or the fishing derby, thinking a casual meeting at a place with a lot of people might be a good idea.

But Tasha doesn't seem to go out much. The women I've dated in the past go to bars or parties. Not Tasha. I never see her anywhere other than the bakery. Maybe I'm getting old and out of practice. At thirty, I've got a few years on her, but something tells me age isn't the issue here.

There's something different about Tasha, something that draws me to her.

"What took you so long?" Jim, my best friend, grumbles as I arrive at the garage.

We've been friends since school and co-own the garage together. I moved here from Maryland after the death of my parents to take Jim up on his offer to buy into the business. My only regret was leaving my younger sister, Kat, back in Maryland, but as fate would have it, she's now relocated here herself, having met and fallen in love with Kurt Urban, a loner who lives in a cabin on the mountain. The two have been inseparable since she moved in with him a few weeks ago. He's a good man and loves her deeply, which makes me happy.

"Well?" Jim demands, pulling me from my thoughts. He's at the front counter, drumming his fingers impatiently on the cash register.

"Well, what?"

He laughs. "You have no fucking clue how badly I need coffee, do you? Hand it over."

I pass him his crazy sweet and creamy coffee and then take one into the office for Brett, the guy we hired to answer the phones and deal with the admin side of things.

"Thanks, Link." He looks up from his screen as I hand him the cup. "Nectar," he declares appreciatively.

I shake my head in disgust. "You two are weird fuckers."

Brett's chuckle follows me to the service counter, where I open the bakery box and take out a strawberry tart. Jim has already polished off one of the blueberry ones.

"So, how's Tasha?" he asks with a big smirk.

Jim came with me for the coffee run last week, and he's been harassing me about her ever since.

I avoid his gaze, taking a bite of my tart. "Fine. Why do you ask?"

"Please. You have a hard-on for the girl a fucking mile wide. Can't say I blame you. She's a sweetheart. I heard Don and Stuart asked her out, and she turned them down. Maybe she's waiting for a better offer," Jim says, giving me a pointed look.

"Matter of fact, I asked her out today. And she said yes," I tell him. Maybe he'll shut the fuck up about it now.

"It's about damn time. I guess she likes dark and brooding."

I glare at him. "I do not brood. I happen to have a brain, unlike you."

I turn away from him and walk toward the work bay, ignoring his chuckle. I've got work to do if I want to get out of here early enough to get in a workout, a shower, and pick Tasha up by 6:30 PM. And I need to decide where to take her.

At 6.25 PM, I'm sitting in my truck outside the bakery. I have a few minutes before I can knock on her door. I have a feeling she won't appreciate me being early. But I need those few minutes to get myself together.

I've never been this nervous about a date. It's been a long time since I took a woman out, but that's not the reason for my nervousness. I've never met anyone like Tasha.

There are no games or agenda with her. She's not trying to impress anyone and what you see is what you get.

I don't think she has any concept of how beautiful she is with her ebony hair, deep brown eyes, and curvy body. I wonder what it would be like to run my hands through her silky hair, to kiss every inch of those delectable curves. I frown as I remember how she pulled her hand away this afternoon. Am I reading her all wrong? We haven't even been on our date yet, and I already know she has the power to wreck me.

I look at my phone and take a deep breath. I have no idea how tonight will go, but I hope I can say and do the right things because the idea of messing it up turns my stomach in knots.

Go slow, I tell myself.

I can't scare her off.

I climb out of the truck and walk around the back of the bakery, pressing the buzzer for her apartment. A few seconds later, she opens the door, and I can't help but stare. I've only ever seen Tasha in her chef's whites with her dark hair pulled back into a bun or a ponytail.

But not tonight.

She's wearing a simple blue dress. There are no embellishments on it, but there's no need when it molds her body so perfectly. Her hair is loose around her shoulders in a silky curtain, and she's wearing lipstick. No, not lipstick. Some kind of shiny gloss. But her cheeks are pink, and she looks ... is she excited to see me?

"Tasha, you look stunning," I say, taking in her glorious curves.

She shrugs. "Thanks. Where are we going to eat?"

"I thought we'd try the Asian place out by the highway. I've made reservations."

She shakes her head. "I can't eat Asian. Too much MSG."

"Oh, I'm sorry. Is there somewhere else you'd like to eat?" I feel like a fucking idiot. I should've asked her if she has allergies.

"Granger's would be better," Tasha replies. "They make most of their food from scratch and don't use a lot of additives."

Grangers isn't exactly what I would call a romantic venue for a date. It's bright, and a lot of truckers go there for the cheap food. But if that's what she wants, that's where we'll go. I'll go anywhere if it means I get to spend some time with this goddess.

I nod. "Sounds good to me."

I open the passenger door of my truck for her. It's a little higher than she's likely used to, and she stumbles a little. I catch her and guide her up with my hand on her hip. She stiffens a little but doesn't say anything. Some women might stumble on purpose, but not Tasha. It wouldn't occur to her to fake something like that for attention. If anything, attention is the last thing she craves.

We drive to Granger's mostly in silence. I can't tell if she's nervous or doesn't want to be here. I hope it's not the latter.

Inside, I spot a booth in the back and guide Tasha toward it. It's not romantic, but at least there won't be people surrounding us.

The server comes and tells us the specials. It's not the impression I was hoping to make. I wanted Tasha to be impressed with a great menu, but she doesn't seem to need that. She orders a tossed salad without dressing and chicken breast with rice. No sauces. It seems like food doesn't matter to her the way baking does.

After ordering the food, I struggle to find questions that interest her. I feel like I'm not asking the right things because she looks bored.

"Tasha, why don't you talk about whatever you like to talk about? I feel like I'm making you uncomfortable, but I want to get to know you," I say after a long pause in the conversation.

She sighs. "I'm not good at this, Link. It's why I don't go out very often. Most people find me ... boring."

"Believe me, boring is the last word I'd use to describe you," I say softly.

"Why?" she asks bluntly.

"Because you're not like anyone else I've ever known. You're not fake. I think you're the most genuine person I've ever met."

She's quiet for a minute, chewing on her bottom lip. "I'm just me, Link. I'm not very interesting. I don't have an exciting life. I bake. You know that. It's my passion. And I don't do much other than watch television with George."

A surge of jealousy hits me in the gut. "George?"

"My cat."

I breathe a sigh of relief. "So, you like to bake, and you like cats. That's something," I say, smiling at her. "Tell me about that. What do you like about baking?"

"I like that there are rules. Baking isn't like cooking. With cooking, you can change the ingredients or the measurements. You can skip ingredients or add more of what you like. I feel like I'm not in control when it comes to cooking. But with baking, so long as I stick to the recipe and follow the rules, the result is always the same. Sometimes the recipes vary slightly, but I always stick with the directions. It's all about the right combinations of ingredients and the right timing. I can control that."

I pause before speaking. I don't want to say the wrong thing. "So, you like being in control?"

A small frown pleats her brow. "Kind of, yes. But there's more to it than that."

"Tell me."

"When someone eats something I've baked, I can see their reaction immediately. They either like it, which makes them happy, or they don't. When it comes to cooking meals, people say things like 'it's too salty' or 'there's not enough spice,' even though I followed the recipe. With baking, so long as you stick to the recipe, people generally like it."

"So, you don't like it when people don't like what you've made?"

She shakes her head, wrinkling her nose. "No. It's not that. I don't like it when I can't tell how people feel about things."

I'm starting to understand Tasha a little bit more. She has a hard time reading people. Is that why she doesn't react how I expect her to when I flirt with her? Is it possible she doesn't understand I'm trying to show her I like her?

Once I've got Tasha talking, she doesn't stop. I learn about her parents, who still live in Medicine Bow and supported her dream to open her bakery. She tells me all about George and how she found him when he was a kitten and took him in. Tasha tells me how he was sick, and she took him to the vet, who told her she had to feed him with a syringe every hour on the hour. And that's precisely what she did.

But the funny thing is, Tasha doesn't ask much about me. Occasionally, I slip in something, but she doesn't react much. With anyone else, I might think they were being rude, but somehow, I know that's not the case with Tasha.

We eat, she talks, and I listen. Which is fine because I love hearing her husky voice as she shares more about herself. She doesn't brag or try to impress me. There's nothing fake or superficial about Tasha. Yet, she's a mystery to me.

Finally, she looks at her watch. "I should go."

I look at my phone and realize it's quarter to nine. "Okay. Let's get you home."

I pay the bill, and we head out to the truck. It's only a short drive back to the bakery, and as I pull up outside, I know I'm not ready for the evening to end.

I turn to look at her as I cut the engine. "What happens at nine?"

"My favorite crime show."

My eyebrows rise. "A television show?"

She nods, pressing her plump lips together as if she's embarrassed.

I'm relieved. I thought it might be a phone call from a long-distance boyfriend or something. Of course, now I know Tasha a little better, I know she wouldn't have gone on a date with me if she had a boyfriend.

"Would you like company? I'd like to see this show that's so important you have to be home in time to watch it."

She tips her head to the side, looking at me for a second. "I guess that would be okay."

Chapter 3
Tasha

I don't know why Link wants to watch my show with me, but it'll be great to have company. I haven't had anyone up to my little apartment since I moved in. Jessica, the sheriff's assistant, used to live here before she married the deputy sheriff, Connor Banks. They live on the outskirts of town now, but Jessica comes into the bakery regularly for Connor's favorite—my triple chocolate chip muffins.

Link follows me through the front door and up the stairs, hanging his jacket on the back of the chair. I want to tell him to hang it up because that's not the place for jackets and coats, but I bite my lip, trying to ignore it.

My apartment is small, with one bedroom, a decent-sized living area, and a separate kitchen, but it suits me perfectly. It's cozy and safe.

"Have a seat," I say to Link, indicating the sofa. "I usually have hot chocolate and a snack while I watch. Would you like some?"

"Sure."

"The remote is on the coffee table. Can you turn it to channel forty-three?" I ask as I head into the kitchen.

I've got enough time to make the hot chocolate before it starts. I don't want to miss the introduction because sometimes there are important hints about the crime, and I like to figure it out.

As I heat the milk, I think about our night. When Link asked me to dinner, I thought he was just looking for someone to eat with. Company. Now, I realize this is a date. Link likes me. And that makes me nervous.

I've never had a serious boyfriend. I've dated, but they ended badly because ... well, I'm different. Not in a bad way. Just different.

We're all unique, and that's beautiful.

My parent's words come back to me. I guess I was a little too unique for the three men I dated in the past. They may have considered me beautiful before the date, but that changed within the first hour. I never heard from any of them again.

I don't know how to flirt or make men feel like they're the most important thing in the world. Which is what most of them seem to want.

When I get nervous, I talk too much and forget to ask questions about the person I'm with. That's usually enough to make them never call me again. But Link hasn't reacted like that. He wants to spend more time with me. He doesn't want to leave.

As I pour the steaming hot milk into the chocolate, it occurs to me that I don't want Link to leave either. I want him to like me. I want him to stay.

I might even want him to touch me. Pulling my hand away this afternoon was an instinctive reaction. I'm not accustomed to tactile contact, but his hand felt good on mine. Better than good, just like when he steadied me with his hand on my hip as I stumbled getting into his truck. It scared me a bit, but all afternoon, I found myself wondering what it would be like if he touched me in other places.

I return to the living room to find Link sitting in the middle of the couch. I place the mugs of hot chocolate and a plate of cookies on the coffee table.

"Those look good," Link says.

"They're macadamia and white chocolate."

He frowns. "I didn't see these in the display at the bakery."

"No, I just made them for me," I tell him. "They are my favorite."

He laughs. "You really do like baking."

Is that funny? I laugh to be polite.

The introduction to the show starts, and we stop talking. I try to focus on the introduction, but I'm having a hard time concentrating because his arm is along the back of the couch behind me. Is he going to put it around my shoulders? Then, it dawns on me that I want him to. I want him to touch me again.

He's being cautious, though. I think I might have messed up when I pulled my hand away.

Just watch the show, Tasha, I tell myself. *Don't worry about it.*

But I can't help myself. Halfway through the show, I realize I'm not even trying to figure out who the killer is because all I can think about is Link beside me. I like him, and by now, I know he likes me, too. I need to find a way to let him know how I feel.

For the next half-hour, I sit there and worry about what I should be doing. How do I tell him I want him to like me?

I sit until the show credits are rolling. Finally, I turn to him and do the only thing I know how to do—be direct.

"Do you want to kiss me?" I blurt.

He looks a little startled. Damn. That probably wasn't the right way to go about it.

"Very much. But I wasn't sure if you liked me that way."

"I-I do like you that way," I reply, wondering why my lips are suddenly dry.

Link's blue eyes darken at my response, and he leans toward me. My heart is racing out of my chest, but I close my eyes like I know I should and wait.

And wait.

I'm about to open my eyes and pull away when I feel his lips on my forehead, on my cheeks, and finally, on my lips. It's not what I was expecting. It doesn't measure up to my limited experience of rushed kisses, which made me uncomfortable.

Link continues to kiss me slowly and gently. His tongue licks across the seam of my mouth, and I open up to admit its warm thrust into my mouth. He tastes like hot chocolate and macadamia, a combination that appeals to me greatly.

He guides me to lay back against the arm of the couch, and he fits his body to mine, raining kisses along the length of my neck. It's a lot, but it feels good, and I don't want him to stop like I did with the other men I dated.

His hand cups my breast through my dress, and he slides a thumb across my nipple. I jolt a little in surprise at the sensation that spirals down between my legs.

"Look at me, Tasha."

I open my eyes. His blond hair is tousled, his cheeks flushed, and his blue eyes are heavy with something.

Desire? I'm a little overwhelmed by the sensations running through my body, but I don't want him to stop. I just don't know what to do or how to act.

"Do you want me to go home?" he asks.

I shake my head. "No. Don't. Stay. Keep going."

He cups my face in his hand. "You're beautiful, Tasha. I want to make you feel as amazing as you make me feel."

I make him feel amazing? Huh. I need to work out how I did that so I can do it again.

But not now because he's touching me again, using his mouth and his hands in ways that make me feel amazing, just like he promised.

He slides the straps of my dress down my arms, and I lift so he can remove my bra, leaving me bare from the waist up. This is already further than I've gone with any man, but I don't feel threatened or rushed. I know if I ask him to stop, he will. But I don't want him to stop. I want more of these new sensations coursing through me.

I can feel his hardness against my thigh. I know if I don't tell him to stop, we're going to have sex. A part of me is nervous, but I know Link isn't like those other men. He cares about what I want. He wants me to enjoy it, and knowing that makes me feel safe. It makes me want what he wants.

I don't say anything else. I lie still and let him do what he's supposed to do. At least what I think he's supposed to do. His hand moves between my thighs, sliding under my panties to touch me intimately. Okay, now, I'm freaking out a bit. I'm breathless, and something is building inside me. I can't let go, but I don't want him to stop. There's a need for some kind of release that makes me uneasy and excited at the same time. I stay silent because I'm not sure what I'm supposed to do.

Suddenly, Link's hand is gone, and he pulls back to look at me, his blue eyes boring into mine. "You're not enjoying this, are you?"

I stare back at him. Did I do something wrong? Was I supposed to act a certain way?

I open my mouth, shaking my head as I try to find my words.

Link gets to his feet, running a hand through his hair. "I'm sorry. I thought you wanted this, too," he says, waving a hand between us.

I grab my dress, pulling it back up to cover my exposed breasts. "I-I do, Link."

One corner of his mouth tips up in a smile, and I wonder what I said that amused him. This doesn't feel like a lighthearted situation.

"You could've fooled me, Tash," he says, his tone harsher than I've ever heard.

"I didn't ... I don't want to fool you, Link. I just—"

"I should go," he says, cutting me off.

I don't want him to, but it seems like he does. I instinctively feel like I did something wrong. But what? He was making me feel so good, and then he stopped. I want him to touch me some more, but maybe that's not how it works. I don't know. I have nothing to compare it to.

I nod.

He puts on his coat and moves toward the door, his hand hesitating on the door handle. He turns back to look at me. "Are you okay, Tash?"

"I'm fine," I say, even though I'm not sure I am.

He gazes into my eyes for a long moment as if he's trying to work something out. He leans in, kisses my forehead, says goodnight, and then he's gone.

I miss him immediately. I screwed it up. I don't have a chance with him anymore. The first tear drips off the end of my chin, followed by another and another.

I go upstairs to my room and change into my pajamas. I can still smell Link on my skin, where he held me close and kissed me. I don't usually like scents other than my own on my skin, but this feels different. I don't want to wash him away because it's comforting, like he's still with me.

I go back downstairs to get the cups and put them in the dishwasher. But before I leave the living room, I lean down and smell the back of the couch. It still smells like him. Kind of sweet, kind of spicy. Not cologne. Just a clean, soapy smell.

I shake my head. I like him. Too bad I messed it up. I make a mental note to watch more romance movies. I need to learn how to act right if I want to have someone like Link in my life. No, not someone *like* Link. I want *him*. Period.

But he's gone.

I head back upstairs, crawl into bed, and cry myself to sleep.

Chapter 4
Link

I drive around for a long time after I leave Tash's apartment. I shouldn't have kissed her tonight. It was too soon. But when she asked me so bluntly, so honestly, I couldn't resist.

I fucking loved touching her, kissing her. I tried to please her, to go so slow. I could tell she was inexperienced. She didn't know what to do. All I wanted was to bury myself inside her, to have that connection with her, claim her as mine from the inside out. Not for one night but for all the nights to come. Her pleasure was my primary focus, but when she didn't respond to my touch, it was clear she didn't feel the same way.

She didn't speak, didn't make any noises as I kissed her breasts and sucked on her nipples. She didn't caress me or clutch me to her or wrap her legs around my hips like a woman who wanted to have sex. She *seemed* relaxed, but her lack of interaction told me in no uncertain terms that she wasn't feeling it. And one thing I'll never do is take advantage of a woman in that way.

I'm by no means a player. I've been with three women in my almost thirty years on this planet. I'm not the most experienced guy in the world, but I know that sex should be a mutual pleasure and that a man always comes after he's satisfied his woman. But Tash was nowhere close to that kind of pleasure. It's humbling, knowing my touch did nothing for her.

I drive past the bakery one more time. Seeing the light on upstairs, I pull over to the side of the street for a minute. I fleetingly think about knocking on her door. Something was off. I need to know what I did wrong. Should I go and talk to her?

The light upstairs goes out, giving me my answer.

I've been falling for Tasha a little more every day, and this isn't how I envisioned our date ending. I'm not sure how, but I screwed up. I have to find a way to make it up to her.

I go to Valentine's Kitchen the next day to see her, but she's not there. Alexa tells me she's sick. I've never known Tasha to be sick a single day in the six months she's been here. Guilt grips my gut, knowing it's because of me, because of last night. I'm the asshole who rushed her into something she wasn't ready for.

I call her, but she doesn't pick up, so I text her, asking if she needs anything. She still hasn't replied by the end of the day, by which time I'm cursing a blue streak at anything and everything.

I make a detour past the bakery on my way home. I'm late finishing work and the place is in darkness. Heading around the back, I press the buzzer and knock on the door, but there's no reply. I'm starting to get worried that she really is sick and needs help before dismissing that idea. Alexa and Lisa were downstairs all day if she needed them. It's me she's avoiding.

I climb back into my truck, drumming my fingers on the steering wheel as I debate what to do. Breaking her door down seems a bit excessive, even though the caveman in me wants to do just that.

My phone pings in my pocket, and I pull it out, my heart jumping as I see I have a text from Tasha.

Please leave. I'm fine. Last night was a mistake. Let's just be friends.

That's it? That's all she has to say? I glance up at the window to see her standing there. She quickly steps back and drops the blind. Now I feel like a fucking stalker.

Anger claws up my chest, and I gun the engine, heading home.

"What the fuck is wrong with you?" Jim demands when I drop the wrench I'm using on the transmission gear nuts for the fourth time. "You've been a miserable fucker for the last three days."

"Don't wanna talk about it," I mutter, trying to keep my attention on the vehicle and not think about the ebony-haired, dark-eyed woman who seems to be invading my every waking moment.

I lie on the creeper and slide under the truck I'm working on, but Jim's having none of it. He grabs my booted feet and pulls me back out, glaring down at me.

"You may not wanna talk about it but there's no fucking way I'm working another minute with your grouchy ass. Now, spill before I smack you across your thick skull with that wrench," he says, pointing at my hand where I'm gripping it so tightly my knuckles are white.

I release a resigned breath, knowing my friend won't drop it until I talk to him. I've been stomping around the workshop in a black mood for the last three days. At this rate, I'll lose our customers. I even snapped at my good friend and the Deputy Sheriff, Connor Banks, when he stopped by yesterday to get a new tire for his cruiser.

"What's going on, Link? Did you and Tasha have a fight? Did your date go badly?" Jim asks.

"You could say that," I grunt.

Jim frowns. "What the hell, dude? You've been head over heels for that woman since the minute you first clapped eyes on her. You go on one date with her, and you're done?"

I push myself to my feet, my eyes blazing fury at him. "No, I'm not fucking done! But you have no fucking idea what—" I force myself to stop. I'm not having this conversation, not here, not now.

"You need to get your ass over there right now and get your shit in order. That woman deserves more than the silent treatment from you."

My lip pulls back in a snarl. "I'm not the one giving the silent treatment. She is."

"Does it matter? I've been doing the bakery run for the last two days because you're too goddamn stubborn to work things out like a real grown-up. I'd put my foot up your ass if your head weren't in the way. Now, why don't you put us all out of our misery, get your ass up there and tell her how you feel, or I'll drag you there," Jim threatens.

Jim and I have been friends for years. I know he means well, but he doesn't get it. "First, try it and see what happens. And second, it's not that simple."

Jim's eyes narrow on me. "You have feelings for her, don't you?"

I nod, blowing out a frustrated breath.

"Then what's the fucking problem?"

I close my eyes as the anger seeps from me. "I screwed it up. I don't know how, but I can't face her."

"Why? Did the date go bad? Did you have crappy sex?"

I glare at him. "Not that it's any of your fucking business, but no, we didn't have sex. We started to and"—I blow out another breath, my cheeks heating with embarrassment—"she didn't react to anything I was doing. I went slow. I asked if she was okay. But she didn't … well, she didn't act as if she liked it."

"Dude," Jim says with a sigh. He shakes his head, his eyes sympathetic. "Your ego took a bashing, huh?"

"Not just my ego," I reply. "It goes much deeper than that. Tash is different, in a good way. I'm drawn to her, but it's like she's got this wall up, and I don't know why."

"Well, there's only one way to find out," he says, raising a dark eyebrow at me.

"I know. I know. Okay. I'm going," I say sheepishly.

"Fuck, what was that popping noise?" Jim asks suddenly, looking around the garage.

"What the fuck are you talking about?" I look at him, wondering if he's lost his mind. "There was no noise."

Jim claps a hand on my shoulder, his face splitting into a wide grin. "Ah, don't worry. It was just the sound of you pulling your head out of your ass at last."

I give him a look of disgust. "Very funny, asshole."

After freshening up in the staff bathroom and putting on the clean shirt from my locker, I walk the few blocks to Valentine's Kitchen. I see Tasha through the window as I pace back and forth on the sidewalk, letting several people go in ahead of me.

Jim was right. I need to talk to her. The feelings I have for her are once in a lifetime. It's not only physical. It's all-encompassing and more than attraction. There's something about her, and I can't—I *won't*—let her slip away.

Finally, I walk through the front door. Tasha sees me right away, and she turns and dashes out the back door.

My heart sinks.

Fuck. I've already lost her.

No. I'm not leaving without a fight, even if it turns out I'm not what she wants. Even if she never wants to see me again, I need to find a way to make things okay for her.

I head out the front door and around the back of the building, finding her leaning against the wall, head back, breathing slowly.

"Tasha…"

"Link, go away. I got the hint. You don't have to say anything. Just forget that night ever happened," she says, not looking at me.

"I don't want to forget it, Tasha. I want to understand. Having you in my arms, kissing you, it was beautiful. *You're* beautiful and kind and genuine. I need you to know that I'm sorry. Sorry if I rushed you or made you feel bad because you don't want me the way I want you." I pause, running an agitated hand through my hair.

"*You're* sorry? For what?" she asks, looking genuinely confused. "It's me who screwed it all up."

"What? Tasha, no—"

"Link, you don't have to lie to me," she says, cutting across me. "I know I'm not like other women you've dated. I've never been with a man, so I don't know what to do in bed. I have a hard time just ... functioning from day to day. I know it's hard for people around me, and I know you're not a mind reader—"

"Tasha, it's not you." It's my turn to cut her off. I reach for her hands, relieved when she doesn't pull away, giving me the courage to go on. "I don't understand what happened. Or what *didn't* happen. I wanted to show you how I felt about you the other night. I wanted to make you feel good. But you didn't say a thing. You didn't moan. You didn't tell me what you liked. You ... well, I figured you were inexperienced or that you were putting up with me, with my touch. But I should have figured it out, and I'm sorry I didn't. I'm in this for the long haul if you'll have me. If it's what you want."

There. I said it. I've handed her all the power—the power to tear me to shreds emotionally.

Silence stretches between us, and when she doesn't reply, I give a small nod and turn to leave.

"Link, wait."

I turn back to face her, and my heart breaks at the pain etched on her beautiful face.

"I ... I n-need to tell you something," she stutters, her brown eyes full of fear.

I move closer, wanting to pull her into my arms but know that's not the best thing for her right now. "You can tell me anything, Tasha. No judgments here. Not ever," I say, capturing her gaze with mine so she can see the sincerity of my words.

She holds my gaze for a moment, searching my eyes as if trying to figure something out. "I-It's not you. It's me. All the things I told you over dinner the other night are true, but ... there's a reason for it. I have Asperger's," she states, pressing her lips together and staring at me with mournful eyes.

I'm confused. "Asperger's? Isn't that a type of autism? You can't be autistic. You run your own business. You graduated from culinary school."

"I'm high-functioning. Most people think I'm odd … but all the little things you mentioned, they're part of having Asperger's. I … I don't communicate very well. I talk too much, or I don't talk at all because I don't understand the physical signals others take for granted. Remember how I told you I like baking because I can tell when people like it? They're happy and show obvious signs, but more importantly, they say what they're feeling. But people aren't always obvious. I wasn't even sure if you liked me until I asked if you wanted to kiss me." Tasha finally comes to a halt as she runs out of breath.

I shake my head, trying to absorb everything she's telling me. "So, you didn't know how I felt? Even though I asked you out on a date? And you didn't realize I was flirting with you?"

Tasha shrugs. "Like I said, I process things differently. I don't pick up on physical cues like flirting. When I was a kid, I had a hard time at school. At first, my parents kept telling me to 'pull my socks up.' I had no clue why the position of my socks would improve my grades," she says, biting her lip and fiddling with the buttons on her shirt. "I don't know how to make small talk. It throws me when someone deviates from the script in the bakery or anywhere. I get all tongue-tied and don't know what to say." She pauses, looking up at me. "But it's okay, Link. You don't have to worry about it. I understand it's a lot to deal with, and I don't expect you to figure it out."

I reach for her hand, and she comes willingly as I pull her toward me. "What if I want to figure it out?" I ask softly. "I'm not gonna lie. It's a lot to take in. But you know what?"

She shakes her head, looking up at me with those soft brown eyes that melt my insides. I take a breath, choosing my words carefully so she won't have to worry about physical cues.

"You're worth it, Tash. Whatever it takes, whatever I need to do to be in your life, I'll do it. I want the chance to ask the right questions and to learn how to communicate so we can understand each other better. Will you let me do that?"

She gives me that long look like she's trying to figure out if I'm being genuine. Finally, she smiles and nods. It's the most beautiful smile I've ever seen because it's aimed at me.

I bring her hand to my mouth and place a kiss against her knuckles. "I'd like to cook for you."

Her smile grows bigger. "Okay."

I let out a relieved breath. "Tonight? I'll pick you up and take you back to my place. We'll talk and eat, and anything else is up to you."

Chapter 5
Tasha

After Link leaves, I try to process the sensations rumbling around my stomach. Is it hope? Acceptance? I know I pushed him away the last few days. I find it difficult to process my emotions, and after our date, I was sick to my stomach, agonizing over what went wrong.

Apart from my parents, Belle is the only person who understands me. But now I think Link wants to understand me, too. That's what he said, right?

I spend the rest of the afternoon getting lost in my preparations for the next day. When Lisa shows up for the evening shift, I tell her, "I'm going to be out tonight, but I'll take my cell phone with me. But only call me if there's an emergency."

"Of course. Do you have a date?" Lisa asks with a big smile.

I feel a smile pulling at my mouth. "Yes, I have a date."

And this time, I know it's a real date.

Link picks me up at seven o'clock and drives me to his house, which is much bigger than I expected.

I look around the large, open-concept main floor. The living room merges with the dining room, and the kitchen is at the far end of the house. His place smells good. Homely.

I turn to face him as he takes my jacket. "Why is your house so big? Is it only you who lives here? Were you married before? Do you have kids? What are you cooking?"

He laughs and shakes his head.

"Sorry." I grimace, knowing I've asked too many questions at once.

"Don't be sorry," he replies, his eyes crinkling up at the corners as he smiles. "Sit down in the living room, and I'll bring you something to drink before I answer all those questions. What would you like? Wine? Water? Hot chocolate?"

"You have hot chocolate?" I ask in surprise.

"I bought some before I went back to work earlier today. I wasn't sure if that was just a crime show drink or if you like it all the time."

Warmth fills my stomach at the knowledge that he went out of his way to get my favorite drink. "I like it all the time."

"Great. Sit down wherever you're comfortable, and I'll bring it to you. Then I'll answer any question you like," he says with a wink that makes my stomach flutter in a different way.

I go into his living room and look at the sofa and the chairs. I choose one of the chairs, knowing I'm not ready to have him sit too close to me yet. His presence is too distracting.

He comes in a few minutes later and places two cups of hot chocolate on the table beside me, and then sits in the chair on the other side of the table.

"Okay, I'll answer the questions you asked first. I'm not married, have never been married, and don't have kids. But I want kids. A lot of them. Which is why I bought this place. I have a sister called Kat who lives beyond the mountain pass with her fiancé, Kurt. Our parents died three years ago in a car crash. There are no living grand-parents, so Kat and I only have each other. When my mom and dad died, I realized I wanted a big family, so my kids wouldn't be alone if anything ever happened to me. I chose this house, hoping that someday it would be filled with a big family. Oh, and dinner is roast pork with potatoes and carrots. I saw what you ordered the other night, and I guessed you prefer simpler foods."

I take a moment to absorb everything he's told me. "Do you want to have children right away?"

I'm not sure if I can manage kids and the restaurant right now. I stop my thoughts before they run away from me. Link didn't say he wanted kids with me.

"I want love, first and foremost. The kids will come when we're both ready."

He said, "we." Does he mean him and me? I clamp my mouth shut, not knowing how to ask.

"Tash, tell me what you're thinking. You look worried," Link says softly. "I promise, you can't say anything wrong. Not to me."

I'm pretty sure that's not the case, based on past experience, but I trust Link not to laugh at me. "When you say 'we,' are you talking about us?"

"I hope I am because I want there to be a 'we' more than anything. I know you think you're different, but so am I. You're a breath of fresh air. You're teaching me things about myself, breaking down habits and barriers I never knew *I* had. I get that you prefer to have words to base your opinions and thoughts on, but it's something I need to practice." Link pauses, capturing my gaze. "Kat, my sister, lost her hearing as a kid following a nasty ear infection. As a family, we had to learn to communicate with her in a whole new way. We all learned ASL so we could sign with her."

My eyes widen on his face. "Your sister is *that* Kat? The one who's setting up a group in the town hall to teach people to sign?"

Link nods. "Yeah, that's her. I'm not sure how much call there is for that kind of thing here in Garland, but it's important to her to raise awareness."

"That's such a great thing to do."

Link smiles. "Ironically, physical cues are important for Kat as she relies on those heavily. But the one thing Kat's situation taught me was that learning a new form of communication isn't an obligation or a chore when the person you're doing it for is someone you care for very deeply."

Again, there's that warm feeling in my stomach, only more intense this time. I can't put a name to it yet, but I know I want to feel it again and again.

We talk a while longer before Link suggests we eat. As I sit at the table, he serves up the food, and as we eat, we talk some more. Link is specific in everything he says. There's no guesswork on my part. And that gives me the courage to engage fully in the conversation. Sometimes, my words come out awkwardly, but he simply asks me to say it in a different way if he doesn't understand.

After dinner, we clear away the plates, and I help him put the dishes in the dishwasher before making ourselves comfortable in the living room again. This time, I sit on the sofa.

"May I," he asks, indicating the spot next to me.

It seems odd for him to ask me, considering it's his house, but I appreciate it nonetheless.

I nod. "Sure."

He sits down next to me but doesn't make any move to touch me, which leaves me with a vague sense of disappointment.

"So, does anyone else in town know about your Asperger's?" Link asks.

I shake my head. "I've always been careful about who I share my diagnosis with. My parents know, obviously, and my best friend, Belle. I know there are times when I should tell people, you know, like when I signed up for my culinary course, I put it on the form. Molly, the woman who trained me, never treated me any differently, but her knowing made communication between us so much easier."

Link nods. "Like learning to sign made communicating with Kat so much easier. It's not up to you to try to fit into some social norm, Tash. It's up to others to educate themselves. I want to learn all I can about autism, about the everyday struggles it brings, so you and I can move forward. Together. Because the one thing I'm sure of is that I'm meant to be with you, and you're meant to be with me."

I stare into Link's blue eyes, and a memory tickles my brain—a question I asked my parents when I was little.

How do I know what someone is thinking? If they mean what they say?

My mom told me there wasn't a way to know. That people use different physical cues to speak their truth without words, but they were unique to every individual. So, sometimes, I was just going to have to trust my gut.

I never understood that. My gut was my stomach, and how could that tell me what someone was thinking or what they were saying?

But now, for the first time, I understand. Because Link's words echo how I feel. From the moment I met him, I knew I could trust him.

Taking a breath, I reach for his hand and curl my fingers around his.

"Would you like me to drive you home now?" Link asks, his voice husky.

I shake my head. "No."

"Would you like to watch TV?"

Another shake. "No."

He pauses. "Would you like to go to bed?"

I smile. He asked a direct question. This I can deal with. "Yes."

He brings our joined hands to his mouth and places a kiss on my knuckles. Then he stands and pulls me gently to my feet before leading me upstairs to his room.

"I'm going to make this so good for you, Tash. I know I almost blew it the last time we were together like this," he murmurs, pulling me close.

"No, you didn't. Having your hands on me made me … happy. And shaky," I whisper, not sure how else to put it.

He places his fingers under my chin and tilts my face up to his. "Have you ever had an orgasm?"

Oh! Another direct question, but this one has the color running up my neck into my cheeks. "I … You made me feel good the other night, but it was as if there should've been more. So, I guess the answer is no. I don't think I've ever had an orgasm."

He releases a breath and shakes his head, a smile pulling at his mouth. He looks at me, noting my confusion at his expression. "No, sweetheart. I'm not laughing at you," he says, smoothing his hands up and down my arms. "I'm laughing at myself. It never occurred to me you may not have had one before. Trust me. Tonight, you will, and you *will* know what it feels like."

Link lowers his head to mine, kissing me softly, gently. An unknown emotion wells up inside me, and I try to decipher it. I feel … safe. For the first time in a long, long time, I'm safe. Here, in this man's arms.

"I want you to try something tonight," Link says, twining his hand with mine and tugging me toward the large bed. "I want you to tell me when you like something and when you don't. There are no expectations. Everyone is different. But the only way I can tell if you're enjoying something is if you tell me. Can you do that?"

"I'll try. If you want me to," I say, nerves fluttering in my stomach. No, not nerves. Anticipation.

"You don't have to say words. If you like something, you can sigh, or moan, or gasp, and I'll know to keep doing it."

I nod, feeling a strange warmth invade my limbs at his words.

Link smiles at me, kissing me deeply as he slowly removes my clothing. Each article he takes off gives him more of my flesh to touch, to kiss, to lick. It all feels good, and I let a little sigh slip from my lips.

Looking up at me, he smiles and says, "That's good, Tash. I love hearing you sigh like that. Let's see if I can make you sigh some more."

Once all my clothing is removed, he guides me to lie on the bed and slides between my legs. He's still fully dressed, but I'm completely naked, every inch of me on display for his eyes only.

His finger slips between my thighs and finds a place that sends a jolt of heat through my body. He rubs it, and the heat increases. I know from science classes he's rubbing my clit, but I never expected it to feel like this. It's like what I felt the other night, only a million times better.

Suddenly, his finger is gone. He kisses my thighs, and out of nowhere, my hips take on a life of their own and I lift them toward him, seeking his touch.

"Tell me, Tash. What do you want?"

"More. Of what you were doing. With your fingers," I say breathlessly.

He smiles at me. "I have something I think you'll like even more."

His fingers lightly touch me and I close my eyes, letting the sensations flow through me. Then, there's a different sensation—something hot and wet touching me there, moving up and down my folds. The heat morphs into a kind of electricity that moves through every cell of my body.

I look down to see Link licking me between my legs. And it feels *incredible*. His tongue moves up and down the space between my legs and then circles my clit. My hips press against him and I don't have to consciously think about making noise. I moan loudly. Louder than I mean to. But I don't care because it feels so good.

"Link ... oh ... my ... God," I mutter.

"Do you like that, Tash?" he asks, barely stopping to speak.

"Oh, oh, yes, don't stop ..."

Speaking is too much. I pant as the pressure builds. This is so much better than the other night. I want ... something, and all I know is that Link can give it to me because his tongue is pure magic.

Suddenly, I feel the pressure coming to a peak, and it scares me a little.

As if he senses my hesitation, Link lifts his head and reaches for my hand, linking my fingers with his. "It's okay, sweetheart. What you're feeling is perfectly normal. I'm here. I've got you. Always. Just let go."

He returns to whatever witchcraft he's creating between my legs, and I know I need to allow whatever happens next to just ... happen. All the electricity and heat coursing through my body culminates in the one place I need it the most. I can't stop it, whatever *it* is, even if I wanted to.

Link continues to suck at my quivering flesh and I press myself against his mouth as the electricity reaches its peak. I groan loudly as a sensation unlike anything I've ever experienced washes over me. A sound works its way up and out of my throat, the kind of sound I never knew I was capable of making.

Link grabs my hips, holding them steady as his tongue flicks back and forth, thrusting and twirling around my clit.

My back arches, my nipples hard pebbles as my body shakes and quivers under his ministrations.

Okay. *Now* I know what an orgasm is.

I'm still breathing heavily when Link crawls up beside me, a grin plastered across his handsome face. "Now, *that's* what I call good oral communication."

He leans in to kiss me and I can taste myself on him, an earthy taste that's not unpleasant. I wonder if he tastes the same.

"Did you like that, sweetheart?" he asks, tugging me close and scattering kisses over my eyes, my brow, and my cheeks.

My stomach warms in a different way when he calls me "sweetheart." I nod enthusiastically. "Is that what an orgasm is like for you?"

"I think so. It's hard to compare," he says.

"I want to make you feel like that."

He pulls back to look at me, his blue eyes fixed on mine. "You do, Tash. All the time."

"No. I mean, I want to make you have an orgasm."

He takes my hand and places a kiss on my palm. "We have all the time in the world for that. Tonight is all about you."

"If that's true, then you need to take off your clothes because I want to make you come."

He chuckles and shakes his head. "You're amazing, you know that?"

I frown. "Because I want to make you come?"

"Because you're perfect exactly the way you are," he replies, dropping a kiss on the end of my nose before leaping to his feet to remove his clothing.

I watch as his T-shirt comes off first, followed by his jeans and boxers. I can't take my eyes off him. I lick my lips as Link stands before me, completely naked. He has a beautiful body, all hard muscles and even harder...

"You have a big cock, Link."

I look up to see him grinning from ear to ear. I was only speaking the truth, but my words have obviously pleased him.

"It's much bigger and thicker than any of the anatomy pictures I've seen in textbooks. None of those pictures do your cock justice. Can I touch you? Is there anything you want? What do you like? Do you want me to do the same thing to you that you did to me?"

He steps forward and runs his knuckles along my cheek. "It's all good, Tasha. The fact that you want to touch me makes me feel good."

Link joins me on the bed again. He's so warm and tempting, and I love the sensation of his flesh under my fingertips. I dip my head, running my lips over his shoulders, his chest, his firm abs, kissing and licking every part I can reach. I'm kind of scared of his cock but the temptation to touch it overwhelms my inhibitions. I grasp him in my hand, surprised to discover how firm and strong it feels, like a big muscle.

Link sucks in a breath and I raise my eyes to his, fascinated by the look on his face. "Am I … hurting you?"

"No, sweetheart. It feels amazing," he says, his voice rough.

"You look like you're in pain," I murmur, moving my hand again and watching him closely.

"Tasha," he moans, closing his eyes. His Adam's apple bobs as he swallows hard.

So this is what a man's face looks like when he's enjoying a woman's touch? Wetness pools between my thighs, knowing that it's my touch he's responding to.

I wriggle down so I'm between his legs. "Do you want me to kiss you here? The way you did to me?" I ask, stroking his hard length as I look up at him.

He's watching, smiling at me, but there's a tension around his jaw. "Do whatever you want, Tash. I'll tell you if I don't like it."

A bead of fluid appears on the end, so I do what comes naturally. I lap it up with my tongue. It tastes slightly salty with an unexpected sweetness. I lick his cock from the base of the shaft all the way to the top. When I run my tongue around the top, he moans. My eyes flick to his face. That means he likes it. I do it several more times. Then, I wrap my lips around the top and lower my mouth over him. He moans again, louder this time.

His hands tangle in my hair, and his fingers tighten every time I run my tongue over a particularly sensitive spot. I play with him for as long as he lets me, experimenting with different things and taking pleasure in his groans. I think his scent and the sound of his moans may be my new favorites, even better than the sound and smell of my freshly ground coffee beans.

"Tasha, I don't know how much longer I can hold off," he says roughly several minutes later, his hands reaching for me. "Come here."

I slide up, lying on top of him. I follow my instincts and press a kiss against his mouth. His tongue steals past my lips and delves inside and I meet it with mine, learning another of his tastes.

Link breaks the kiss. "Turn on your side," he says gruffly.

I move to face him, not knowing what to expect, but I trust him. He slides a hand up my leg and hooks it over his hip, opening me up to his thick fingers as he slides them between my folds and circles my clit. I bite my lip and moan, leaving him in no doubt that I like what he's doing.

Link smiles. "There she is. My beautiful, sexy woman. All mine."

I'm still sensitive from my previous orgasm and I jerk and shake under the rhythmic movement of his fingers, digging my nails into his shoulder. I can feel his hardness between my legs as he lowers his mouth to my breasts, sucking and licking at my nipples until I'm gasping and panting as the powerful sensation builds inside me again.

His cock nudges at my entrance, and I tense as fear of the unknown, of being out of control, washes over me.

"How about we try this a different way," Link says, reading my expression once more.

He rolls us so he's on his back with me straddling his hips. His cock stands straight up, angling toward his stomach.

"You're in control, Tash. I want to be inside this beautiful body more than I've ever wanted anything, but you set the pace. If you want to stop, we'll stop, okay?"

I nod, taking him in my hand and positioning him at my entrance. My eyes hold his as I take him inside me, just an inch. The wetness between my legs acts as a lubricant, helping me take him inside me another inch. It feels good and I want more.

I sink down another inch and stop, hissing at the discomfort as he stretches me open in a way I've never experienced before.

"It's okay, sweetheart. You're new to this, so your muscles are tight," he says, moving a hand between us and finding my clit with his thumb.

I jerk and moan as my body opens up to him. His other hand moves to my hip, steadying me, guiding me as I sink all the way down on his length.

I brace my palms against his chest as the pleasure builds once more. I can tell it's going to be even more intense this time, heightened by the movement of his thumb against my bundle of nerves and the connection of his body against mine. It's a kind of connection I've never experienced before, one that's more than physical. As if my heart is linked to him somehow.

Link's hand tightens on my hip as I move against him, feeling him rooted deep inside me. "God, Tasha, you feel so fucking good. I hope I make you feel as happy as you make me. I want to make you feel good forever."

"Yes, yes, Link. I want that, too." I sigh, rolling my hips faster. "I want to hear your orgasm. Like you heard mine."

Link thrusts up as I lower down, and it feels so amazing. His thumb taps against my clit, and my muscles contract around his girth. I want, I need, I *crave* more.

Our bodies are like one, and hearing his excitement works me up even more.

"Tasha, I can't hold back much longer," he rasps, his face flushed, his blue eyes flashing.

I know I can't either. I'm about to explode.

Link surges into a sitting position, grasping my hips with both hands. He takes control and I relinquish it willingly, trusting him completely as he moves me up and down on his length. He buries his face in my neck, nipping at the sensitive skin there.

"Ah, fuck, Tasha!" Link calls out my name over and over as his cock twitches inside me, filling me with his seed.

Seeing and feeling him orgasm sends me over the edge, and my body clenches around him as I explode into a million shards of pleasure.

"Link!" I moan his name loudly, almost sobbing at the intensity of the ecstasy that rocks through me, leaving me weak and floppy as it slowly ebbs away.

I clutch him to me, smoothing my hands through his hair as we both catch our breath. I've never known this kind of closeness, both physical and emotional. It's everything I never knew I needed.

A few moments later, I feel wetness on my cheek. I pull back to look at him, my heart pounding. Moonlight spills through the window, making the single tear on his cheek glisten.

"Link? Are you okay? Did I do something wrong? Was I no good at it? You didn't enjoy it?" I ask in a rush, touching the wetness on his cheek.

Link's arms tighten around me. "I'm more than okay, sweetheart. What you've given me, what we just did, it's more than sex. You trusted me enough to let go completely. You gave me a gift. You let me in and showed me who you really are. And I swear, I'm going to do everything I can to prove to you I am worthy of it."

He kisses me deeply, holding me tightly, and making me feel safe and loved.

Without a shadow of a doubt, I know I have never felt more at ease with who I am in my entire life than I do in Link's arms.

Epilogue
Tasha

One Year Later

I know why we're at the mall.

Link has gotten to know me better than anyone else ever has except for my parents and Belle. He accepts me for who I am, and when he doesn't understand, he doesn't judge, he just asks questions until he works out what I'm trying to say. And then he accepts it and gives me what I need.

That's why Link knew I wouldn't want the traditional kind of proposal. I don't want some crazy engagement ring on a cake with lots of people around. I don't want something I'm not expecting.

So, we talked about it. He proposed at his house, over dinner. No ring. He knew I'd like to choose it.

We went to Spring's Jewelers and picked out the ring together.

"How did he propose?" the woman behind the display counter asks with an indulgent smile. She hands the box to Link, who carefully removes the beautifully simple solitaire engagement ring.

"Over several weeks," I answer, looking up at my fiancé with a smile.

The saleslady gives us a quizzical look. It's clear, even to me, that she doesn't understand. She's probably used to stories of grand gestures from couples when they come to collect their rings. But Link and I understand each other, and that's all that matters.

We leave the mall, the ring on my finger.

"So, time to plan the wedding?" he asks, kissing my hand.

I look up at him. "What do you want?"

Smiling at me, Link says, "I'm happy with whatever you choose. We can have a big wedding, or we can have something small."

"How about having the wedding at Valentine's Kitchen?"

"Sure. Who's going to do the cooking?"

"I'll bake ahead of time. I'll hire someone else to cater," I tell him.

"If that's what you want."

I smile. Link gets me. He even said it was okay if I wanted to wait a year or so before we got married, but I insisted it had to be right away. It'll be a small wedding with only my parents, Belle and her husband, Kat and Kurt, and their baby son, Harry. Just close family and friends. I suggest a date for a month from now.

"Why so fast?" he asks as we approach the truck in the parking lot.

"Well, if we leave it too much longer, I won't fit into my dress."

"Why wouldn't you—" Link stops midstride and turns to look at me. The look on his face is priceless. "Are you...?"

I know I don't like surprises, but he does. I've gotten pretty good at surprising him, but this is the best one.

"Pregnant," I say, finishing his sentence.

"What? How long? You've done a test? When are you due? Do you feel okay? Have you had morning sickness?" The questions roll off his tongue, one after another.

We get in the truck and I turn to face him. "Two months along. Yes, I've done six tests. My due date is Valentine's Day. I'm absolutely fine. I've had a little nausea but nothing major. I hope you don't mind if we find out the gender at our first ultrasound?"

He shakes his head in wonder. "Mind? I can't wait! I hope it's twins!" he declares, pulling me across his lap and kissing me breathless.

He lets me up for air several minutes later, pressing his forehead against mine. "I love you, Tash. So much."

"I love you, too, Link," I reply, feeling that love deep down inside me. It's a well of emotion specifically for my future husband and the father of my children.

He holds my hand all the way home, turning his head to look at me with a satisfied grin at regular intervals.

"Watch the road, mister," I laugh.

"I love you, Tash," he says. "You've made me the happiest man ever. Twice in one day."

I smile at my man, wrapped in dreams of our future together. Link loves me just as I am. We'll always be there for each other, whatever life throws our way because love really does conquer all.

Bonus Scene
Tasha

There's a noise. Not a big noise. A tiny squawk. Like a duckling that's just remembered it forgot to be born. And now it's back. Again.

"Link," I whisper, even though he's already awake and halfway to the bassinet with the kind of silent efficiency that makes me suspect he might secretly be part owl. Or ninja. Owl ninja. Owlja? No, that sounds like a pasta.

I groan and roll onto my back, flinching as sore muscles protest. Apparently, giving birth wasn't a one-time trial-by-fire. No, it's more of a "congrats, your body will now be a misaligned Rubik's cube forever."

My husband lifts our son—*our son*, still wild to think—and cradles him against his bare chest, shushing and bouncing and making low, soothing noises. They sound vaguely like the ocean and warm soup and home. I stare at him in the dim light. His hair is sticking up in five different directions. His eyes are puffy. His jaw is covered in stubble. He looks like a man who wrestled a hurricane and then adopted it.

And he's beautiful.

I start crying. Again.

Link notices, because of course he does. He's got a sixth sense for my tears. Or maybe it's the law of averages because I cry all the time now. For reasons. Or no reasons. Sometimes because the burp cloth is folded wrong.

"Hey, sweetheart." He brings Valentine over and sits beside me on the bed. Yes, we named our baby Valentine; I couldn't *not* when he came into the world on Valentines Day. Apparently, it means strength and health in Latin. "You okay?"

I nod. Lie. Nod again. "I'm just… overwhelmed." And leaky. And tired. And scared. And in love with two humans so deeply it physically hurts.

He rests Valentine in the crook of my arm and kisses my temple. "You're doing amazing."

"That's a strong word. I brushed my teeth today but only because the mint toothpaste smell makes me feel like less of a swamp witch."

"I happen to like your swamp witch energy."

"You like everything I do," I mutter, sniffling.

"Because I love everything you are."

Ugh. He's so *good*. I don't deserve this man. Or this squirmy, blinking bundle with his dark hair and pouty lips who looks way too much like both of us and makes my brain melt on sight.

Valentine sneezes.

I gasp. "Did you hear that? He sneezed like a tiny dragon."

"Pretty sure dragons sneeze fire."

"Maybe he's *part* dragon. That would explain the fussiness. And the unpredictable diaper explosions."

"He's a baby, Tash. That's their MO."

We sit in silence for a bit. Valentine settles down, eyes fluttering shut, mouth opening in that adorable goldfish yawn. My chest tightens with love and fear and more love.

"I'm scared I'm doing it wrong," I whisper.

Link doesn't rush to answer. He never does, not with me. Instead, he adjusts the pillows behind my back and helps me cradle Valentine more comfortably against my chest. "You're not doing it wrong. You're doing it your way. That's more than enough."

"But what if he needs things I don't understand?" I stroke a fingertip over Valentine's downy hair. "What if he cries and I miss the reason? What if he wants a mother who doesn't talk to birds or get overwhelmed by the blender?"

"He's got a mother who sings lullabies about sourdough starters and hand-folds onesies with surgical precision. Who knows the difference between six kinds of cinnamon by smell alone and writes love notes in cookie dough."

He tips my chin up until I'm looking at him, and his blue eyes are ocean-deep and serious.

"Tasha, he doesn't need a different version of you. He just needs *you*. The you who talks to birds and sees the world in patterns. The you who loves him like it's the most natural thing in the world—even when it feels impossibly hard."

More tears.

Link presses kisses to both my cheeks, catching them before they fall. "You're not alone. Not in this. Not ever."

"I know," I whisper. And I do. Even on the worst days. Even when my brain tells me I'm failing. I look at Link and Valentine and somehow, I remember I'm not.

We lie down together, our son between us, our hands tangled over his belly. The world shrinks to this small circle of warmth and breath and quiet love.

Link hums a lullaby. It's off-key and soft, and maybe it's the sleep deprivation talking, but I'm pretty sure it's the theme song to a 90s sitcom. Doesn't matter. My body relaxes against his, and for the first time all day, I feel calm.

Valentine sleeps.

Link watches us both with that steady, unshakeable devotion that makes me believe we're going to be okay.

Better than okay.

"We made a whole person," I whisper, like I haven't said it every day for the past month.

Link smiles and presses another kiss to my forehead. "We sure did, sweetheart. And he's perfect. Just like his mama."

Thank you for reading!

Reviews help readers discover new books! If you enjoyed this book, I'd love to hear what you enjoyed most—your review means the world to me and guides other readers to discover my work.

Thanks for choosing my books—I hope they allow you to relax and escape for an hour or two.

Happy reading!

Love,

Violet.

Keep reading for a sneak peek of Kat & Kurt's story in Dad Bod Mountain Man (Kat is Link's sister), and Claiming Noelle.

Claiming Noelle Sneak Peek

Snowbound with a holiday angel, will his frozen heart finally begin to melt?

Noelle

Like a million other people, I'm headed home to spend time with family for Christmas. But unlike those who make it home for the holidays, I get stuck in a ditch in an unfamiliar small town in Colorado. When a gruff stranger helps me out of my predicament, we both end up stranded in the winter storm...in his cozy, secluded cabin nestled in the trees outside of town.

Callum Stone is a man of few words, and his grumpy demeanor is enough to put most people off, but I see beneath his frosty exterior to the wounded man--a man I'm already falling for.

Callum

I'm still reeling from the sudden loss of my parents a year ago. I don't want to put a damper on everyone else's holiday festivities while I fake my way through the season, so I retreat to my cabin on the outskirts of town to wallow in self-pity. I'm on a tight deadline to finish the book I started before tragedy struck. The last thing I need is to rescue a damsel in distress on my property, even if she does look like a gift-wrapped angel who fell from Heaven.

But as I spend time with Noelle, her gorgeous brown eyes, bubbly personality, and zest for life seep under my defenses, making me realize that there's still something worth celebrating--her.

When the storm passes, and things begin to thaw, will our feelings for each other melt away, too?

Sneak Peek

Noelle

"Let it snow, let it snow, let it snow!" I sing, increasing the volume by pressing the button on the steering wheel.

I love Christmas, and this is one of my favorite songs. I bob side to side as I sing. It doesn't matter that I've heard this song a gazillion times as I belt it out at the top of my lungs.

My ringtone interrupts the song, and I smile as I glance

at the screen on my dash. My cell phone is connected via Bluetooth, so I hit the button to answer the call.

"I'm still a couple of hours away, Mom," I answer Mom's question before she can ask it. She's called me three times since I left home this morning. It's a long journey, and I wanted to make it to my parents in Denver before it gets dark.

"Is it snowing?" Mom's voice comes clearly through the speakers.

I almost laugh at her question. Snowing? It's more like a blizzard. I've been in Utah for the last two years, and it doesn't snow like this.

"Yeah, it's snowing, but it's all good. I'm on the inter-state, and the roads are pretty clear right now."

Visibility is my biggest worry. The windshield wipers are at full speed and still struggling to clear the thick flakes.

"Okay, honey. Drive safe. We can't wait to see you."

"I'll be there before you know it, Mom. Love you."

"Love you, too, Angel," Mom replies, using the nickname she gave me the day I was born—Christmas Day.

Yep, that's right. I share my birthday with the biggest holiday date of the year, and Mom says I was the best Christmas present she ever had twenty-two years ago. She and Dad tried for a baby for years with no success.

They were about to give up and accept that it would only be the two of them when Mom found out she was pregnant at thirty-nine, and I became their Christmas miracle.

Some people might resent it, but I love that I was born on Christmas Day. Mom and Dad have never let the day pass without making it a double celebration and thoroughly spoiling me.

The Sat Nav interrupts my thoughts as the male AI voice tells me to take the next exit. I've nicknamed him George because he sounds just like George Clooney.

"What was that?" Mom asks.

"Just the Sat Nav, Mom. I'll call you back when I'm half an hour away. I need to focus on where I'm going."

I hit the button to end the call. I don't want to worry Mom, but I'm unsure why the Sat Nav is telling me to take the next exit. Don't I usually take the one after? I've only driven this route a few times since moving to Utah for work, but everything looks different with a blanket of snow.

That's when I see it. A sea of red taillights up ahead beyond the next exit. Ah, so that's why George is taking me off at an earlier exit. I shrug. There must be an issue up ahead. If I don't get off the interstate here, I could be stuck in traffic for hours. Big no-no.

I indicate to turn off the interstate and take the exit ramp. Vehicles in front of me are making the same decision, and I leave plenty of room between my car and the vehicle in front. Unease trickles down my spine. I'm taking an unfamiliar route, and visibility is worsening by the minute.

"It's okay, Noelle. You've got this," I tell myself. Better to arrive late than not at all. The light at the bottom of the ramp changes, and the traffic starts moving.

"Turn right," George says.

I frown as the vehicles in front of me turn left. Do they know something I don't? Is George having a senior moment and sending me the wrong way? I check the navigation screen, which has an arrow pointing right.

"Why are we going right, George?"

I know it's silly to talk to a piece of tech. Listening isn't one of George's strengths. He just tells me where to go—literally.

The man in the car behind me honks impatiently and revs his engine, alerting me that I've hesitated a little too long. I gently lift my foot off the brake, let the car drift forward, and carefully apply pressure to the gas pedal. Mr. Testosterone can learn patience. The exit ramp is covered in snow, and I have no idea how slick it is.

I glance in my rearview mirror as I reach the end of the ramp and turn right. My heart skips as I see the vehicles behind me turning left. I'm the only one going in this direction. Not a good sign. Maybe they're all headed somewhere else, and I'm the only one traveling to Denver?

"Trust George, Noelle," I murmur.

I'm half a mile down the road when George says. "Recalculating."

"What? Uh, no, George," I snap, glaring at the navigation screen.

"Turn right in one mile," George announces smoothly.

"Don't think I don't know what you're doing, George," I huff. "Trying to find me a safe spot to turn around, huh?"

I'm the only vehicle on this road stretching in front of me. The verges on either side are piled high with snow. It's been falling here for hours, maybe days, and it's getting worse as I drive. Hopefully, once I've turned around, I'll head to an area with less severe weather.

Suddenly, without warning, the road becomes harder to navigate. Okay, maybe there was one of those signs with curvy lines. I didn't pay much attention. But all the signs in the world won't make me feel better about this drive. Sharp bends in the road and snow doesn't bode well.

Then, as quickly as it goes from straight to curvy, the road evens out again—a long stretch of road with no bends in sight. I let out the breath I didn't realize I'd been holding.

"In five hundred feet, turn right," George says.

"Finally!"

It's okay. I'll quickly turn around, get back on the interstate, and be home free. Maybe the traffic jam will have cleared by then, and I can hop back on. After this little detour, I'd rather take the interstate than—

A moving object launches onto the road. Some kind of animal. A deer? Oh, God. I think it's a baby.

I react instinctively, yanking the steering wheel sharply and missing the fawn by inches. Panic quickly replaces my initial relief when the car careens wildly into a skid.

Don't hit the brakes. Don't hit the brakes.

Sheer terror overrides common sense, and I hit the brakes, sending the car sideways toward a ditch. It seems as if I teeter for an eternity before my little Chevy lands driver's side down in a lump of snow with a bone-jarring *thwump.*

The engine dies. I sit there for a minute, my knuckles white on the steering wheel.

"Okay. It's okay. You're okay," I tell myself.

I try to start the engine again—I'm unsure why because I can't go anywhere.

The engine cranks but doesn't start.

"Great. Fucking great," I mutter.

Even if I could get it started, I'm lodged sideways in a ditch, so unless my little Chevy suddenly morphs into Chitty Chitty Bang Bang and flies me out of here, I'm going nowhere—no fine four-fendered friend coming to my rescue.

A half-hysterical laugh escapes me at the thought as the adrenaline kicks in. I take a few deep breaths to calm my pounding heart and shaking hands.

I look out the driver's window, which is pressed against the bottom of the ditch. I'm going to have to climb out the passenger side. This should be fun.

Pulling my keys from the ignition, I grab my purse, which has somehow ended up dangling by the strap from the rearview mirror. Crossing it over my body, I wriggle into the passenger seat and reach overhead to open the door. It's surprisingly hard to open when it's above my head, but I manage and finally scramble—not so elegantly— from the car.

I haul myself from the ditch and stand on the side of the road, taking a moment to check that all my limbs are intact. My left wrist chooses that moment to throb painfully, and I vaguely remember jarring it on the wheel as I hit the ditch. Thankfully, it's my non-dominant hand, and hopefully, it's just a sprain.

It's mid-afternoon, and the frigid wind cuts through my sweater and jeans, causing me to shiver. My thick winter coat is in the truck, along with my suitcase.

Reaching into my purse, I pull out my phone to call my parents, gritting my teeth as the pain in my wrist increases. No signal. I move around, trying to get at least one bar on my phone, to no avail. Shit. I sigh in frustration. I can't even call a tow truck.

I have no idea where I am. Correction—I'm in the middle of Nowheresville. The only place for miles is a cabin nestled among the trees at the end of a long driveway. I'm getting colder by the minute and need to get out of this wind before I catch pneumonia. My wrist now throbs with the thump of my heart. I pull up my sleeve to see it's starting to swell. I don't think it's broken, but there's no way I can clamber back down the ditch for my coat.

I look around again. Apart from the cabin, there's no building as far as the eye can see. Hopefully, someone will be home. I can use their phone and wait in the warm until the tow truck arrives. My car will be pulled from the ditch, and I'll be on my way. Yes, I'm an optimist—don't judge me.

Decision made, I lock the car and trundle up the long drive to the cabin. I check my phone on the way, praying for a signal, but the bars remain empty. Even if this place doesn't have a phone signal, they'll hopefully have internet. That's if someone is even home. This could be a vacation place. As I approach, there's no sign of a car, but the driveway disappears around the back of the cabin, so maybe it's parked there.

Shivering, I take the porch steps and halt before the front door. I give three harsh raps on the glass and wait. A minute passes with no answer. I knock again. Nothing.

Tentatively, I reach for the door handle. What will I do if it's unlocked? I don't want to add breaking and entering to my list of woes—although I wouldn't technically be "breaking," just "entering."

It's a moot point because the door is locked.

Stepping back, I consider my options. Maybe the back door is unlocked? My hands are numb, and I'm pretty sure I have an icicle forming on the end of my nose. If I can get inside for a little while, I can warm up and form a plan. As it is, the cold is numbing my brain.

I descend the porch steps and walk around to the rear of the property. Spotting the back door, I knock again. No reply. I try the handle. Locked.

"Fuck," I grunt, my breath pluming in the air.

Standing on my tippy-toes, I peek through the window into what looks like a kitchen. I'm about to turn away when a man's face appears on the other side. I shriek and stumble backward, losing my balance and landing in the snow with a thud. The air leaves my lungs in a whoosh, and I lay there gasping like a floundering fish as I stare at the snow-heavy sky.

A door opens, and heavy footsteps scrunch through the snow. I turn my head slowly to see a man approaching.

He's enormous, and he looks pissed. His dark hair falls over his brow, and anger flashes in the deepest brown eyes I've ever seen as he looms over me.

He glares at me like I'm the enemy. "Who the fuck are you, and what the fuck are you doing on my property?"

Dad Bod Mountain Man Sneak Peek

A silent world. A shattered dream. One unexpected love to heal them both.

Kurt

Being a firefighter isn't just a vocation, it's who I am—until an injury on the job sets me on an unfamiliar path. Suddenly, my life has no direction, and my whole future becomes an unfamiliar landscape.

Seeking solace in the mountains of Colorado, I try to put my past behind me and start over. There, I rediscover myself between the pages of the steamy romance novels I write. Stories of men finding the women who complete them fuel my soul, but my empty heart still craves its own happy ending.

So when a blonde-haired angel in need of my help literally tumbles into my path, I know it's no coincidence, and my future suddenly becomes crystal clear ...

Kat

Losing my hearing as a kid left me feeling more discon-nected from the world than ever. I've spent my life looking for something, some*one* who makes me feel whole again—but I never expected to find it in the mountains of Colorado.

During a road trip to visit my brother, I take a nasty tumble and end up in the arms of mountain man, Kurt, who rushes me back to his cabin, single-minded in his mission to save me. His nurturing spirit, attentive touch, and intense gaze make me feel seen and heard in a way I haven't experienced in a long time—if ever.

He thinks he's simply healing my wounds when in real-ity, he's healing his own ... and stealing my heart in the process.

Sneak Peek

Kurt

Dusk was settling in by the time I returned to the cabin. I'd made the hour drive into town to collect the package that had been delivered to the mailing office, not lingering to make small-talk with anyone before heading straight back.

The town of Garland was small compared to Houston, but it still contained far too many people for my liking. I avoided them like the plague these days. I didn't want to see their looks of sympathy when they saw my heavy limp or the scars that marred my right arm and hand. I didn't need their pity, and I sure as hell didn't need their idle chit-chat.

Apart from the occasional hiker that wandered off-trail, I was alone up here. That particular hiker had decided to set up camp on my property. Word quickly reached town about the wild mountain man who'd chased a hiker off his land brandishing an ax. Since then, I'd been left well and truly alone. Not that that particular rumor was accurate—I'd been brandishing a shovel, not an ax. The shovel I kept by the front door to clear the snow, which was still pretty abundant this time of the year.

Being alone suited me just fine. I'd come here for the peace and solitude, to lick my wounds after the accident that had robbed me of the only thing I'd ever wanted to do—the only thing I'd ever wanted to *be*.

No, the only company I needed was my own and that of my German Shepherd, Blaze.

I knew I'd become a grumpy fucker since the accident. It was one of the reasons I'd jumped on the chance to move here. Inheriting my late uncle's cabin had seemed like the perfect solution when I'd been forced to leave my old life behind. And Garland, Colorado, was about as different as I could get from my life in Houston.

The weather, for a start. It was freezing here, a complete contrast to the milder temperatures of the city. Then there was the view. Being a city boy, born and bred, I hadn't expected to like the wide-open spaces and endless views, but there was a beauty and simplicity to life here that had already begun to soothe my broken spirit.

The snow was coming down thickly now, and I was glad to have made it back before the mountain pass was cut off. I had my writing to keep me occupied and enough supplies to last me for months if I got snowed in. Although, this latest storm hadn't been predicted.

As I shouldered my way through the front door and headed toward the kitchen, an almighty boom reached my ears. Blaze whined, and I frowned, setting the heavy box on the worn oak table before venturing back outside. Another boom echoed through the air, followed by the sound of crunching metal. My eyes narrowed on an area of Aspen pines about a half-mile away.

What the...?

A gust of freezing wind hit my face. I tugged up the hood of my heavy coat and headed toward my car with Blaze hot on my heels. I grabbed the flashlight from the glove box and turned it on.

"Come on, boy," I said, and Blaze lolloped along next to me as I headed in the direction of the sound, my heavy boots crunching through the thick snow.

We walked for about ten minutes before I saw the lights flashing on and off through the trees up ahead. I blew out a plume of condensation as I moved closer, shining the flashlight onto a Volvo with rental plates lodged up against the trunk of a huge tree. The whole front end of the car was crushed, and glass and pieces of metal littered the surrounding snow.

The icy wind buffeted me as I trudged through the debris, shining the torch inside the car. It didn't occur to me to hesitate or worry about the gruesome sight that might greet me. I was no stranger to this kind of situation. It was in my DNA to rescue people from danger.

Not anymore, my mind whispered.

Ignoring the depressing thought, I made my way around to the driver's side of the vehicle. The driver's door was open, but there was no sign of the car's occupant. I swung my flashlight in a circle, scanning the immediate area, and the light fell on what looked like a bundle of clothes a little way up the embankment. As I moved closer, it became clear that it was a body slumped on the ground, covered in a fine layer of snow.

A woman, her blonde hair splayed out around her head. It looked as if she'd thrown herself from the car before it impacted the tree, an action that had no doubt saved her life. My eyes ran over her pert little nose with its smattering of freckles and her pillowy-soft lips. She looked like a sleeping angel, fallen from Heaven, but the blood on her forehead told me she was definitely not sleeping.

Unconscious, yes.

Dead, possibly.

The thought made my heart clench painfully. It was an unfamiliar feeling. I'd been involved in all manner of emergencies in the past but something about this woman, her body vulnerable and motionless, affected me deeply.

Shrugging off the strange feeling, I stooped down and placed two fingers against the icy skin of her neck. It took a few seconds before a reassuring pulse flickered against my fingertips, and I breathed a sigh of relief.

I quickly checked her over for broken bones, skimming my hands over her limbs and trying not to notice her abundant curves. I gently ran my fingers across her scalp, feeling for any kind of depression that could indicate trauma to the brain. Nothing. That was good. Although, she had a nasty gash over her left eyebrow that looked like it would need stitches.

I had no way of knowing if she had any internal injuries, but I had to risk moving her—I sure as hell couldn't leave her out here to freeze to death. The nearest hospital was more than three hours away, and this spot was inaccessible to an ambulance.

Blaze danced around me as if telling me to hurry. The snow was falling thicker and faster now, and the wind was a frigid blast against my face.

"Okay, boy. Let's get her back to the cabin."

Blaze barked in agreement. I swore he was more human than canine. He seemed to understand every word I said.

I reached into the car and plucked out the coat dangling off the passenger seat. Her purse was in the footwell, so I grabbed that, too, looping it around my neck. Any other personal belongings would have to wait for another time.

Wrapping the coat around the woman as best I could, I hauled her up into my arms. Carrying unconscious victims was something I'd done easily before my accident. But I'd lost a lot of stamina since leaving the fire service. Between that, my dodgy leg, and the several pounds I'd gained, I wondered if I would be able to carry her the half-mile back to the cabin.

That I even had to ask myself that question pissed me off. Of course, I could get her back to safety, damnit. I was injured, not dead. But the woman in my arms would be if I didn't get her out of these freezing temperatures.

With a grunt, I put one foot in front of the other and set off, ignoring the discomfort in my leg. It took me twice as long to make the return journey, and relief hit me as the cabin came in sight. The woman hadn't so much as twitched an eyelid the whole way back. She had a concussion at the least, but I'd need to check her over more thoroughly once I got her inside. My priority, though, was to get her warm. Her body was like a human popsicle.

Carrying her through to the living area, I placed her gently on the large sofa before quickly lighting the fire. The fireplace was already laid with kindling and logs, so it was just a case of getting it going. Within seconds, the wood was spitting and hissing as the flames poured warmth into the room.

Unlooping the purse from my neck, I tossed it onto the nearby chair and quickly removed my boots and coat. Returning to the unconscious woman, I set about removing her clothes, which were practically frozen to her body. My movements were methodical as I removed her sweater and jeans, careful not to jar or jostle her too much. Seeing her in just her underwear made my stomach clench with desire. I swallowed hard, trying not to notice her full breasts, soft stomach, and thick thighs. She was fucking gorgeous.

But right now, she needed medical attention, not me gaping at her delectable curves like a goddamn pervert. What kind of asshole got hard over an unconscious woman?

Bruises were blooming all over her body, and the area around her left shoulder was already turning a dark purple color—possibly from being thrown against the driver's door or the impact from hitting the hard ground.

There was a vulnerability about her as she lay there, the gash over her eye a stark contrast against her pale face. I wrestled with the strange desire to pull her into my arms and shield her from any further harm.

Forcing myself to focus, I ran my hands over her briskly, grateful for my two years of medical school training before I'd dropped out and transferred to the fire service. I checked again for broken bones and internal bleeding, noting the bruises around her ribs, likely from her seatbelt. Her left ankle was swollen and purpled, although I suspected it was a nasty sprain rather than a broken bone.

Keeping my eyes firmly above her chest, I stripped off her wet bra, deciding at the last minute to leave her panties on. I didn't think my heart would survive the sight of her naked pussy. I wrapped her in the warm blanket from the back of the sofa, breathing a sigh of relief once her tempting curves were hidden from my gaze.

Blaze pattered into the room and slumped down in front of the fire, his ears pricked up.

"Keep an eye on her, boy, while I go grab my medical supplies," I instructed.

Blaze replied with a little woof, moving closer to the unconscious woman. Seemed he was feeling just as protective over her as I was.

I patched her up as best I could, cleaning and stitching up the wound above her eye and bandaging her ankle. I was amazed she hadn't sustained more significant injuries, considering the condition of the car.

I removed my gloves and washed my hands, plucking her purse from the chair and rifling through it. It felt like an invasion of privacy, but I needed to find some form of identification for my injured guest. She might have loved ones looking for her, a husband, maybe. The thought made my chest constrict.

Locating her driver's license, I quickly scanned it. Katherine Thompson. According to the date on her license, she was twenty-four years old and from Maryland. What the hell was she doing here in Colorado, driving alone in a snowstorm? On vacation? Visiting family?

A moan from the sofa had me whirling to face her. Her eyes were still closed, but her brow was creased in pain, and she was shivering uncontrollably, despite the heat from the fire.

"It's okay, Katherine, you're safe," I murmured, moving next to her and gently rubbing my hands over her limbs through the blanket to warm her up.

Her eyes flickered open, revealing a pair of the bluest eyes I'd ever seen. "So c-cold," she rasped as another shudder wracked her body. Her eyes closed again, but her body still shook uncontrollably.

I needed to warm her up. Fast. And there was only one way I could think of to do it.

About the Author

Loved this book?

Find more steamy romances from Violet Rae:

www.authorvioletrae.com

Violet Rae writes spicy, emotionally charged romances where the connection is instant, the heroes are protective (and a little bit unhinged for their woman), and the heat level threatens to set off smoke alarms. From fated mates in outer space to small-town rescues and paranormal standoffs, Violet's stories deliver fast love, fierce devotion, and that delicious fantasy of being utterly cherished.

There's always a woman in danger (or simply in need of a serious nap), a hero who will burn down the world for her, and just enough humor to make you snort-laugh between kisses and kidnappings. Found families, caretaking intimacy, dirty talk, and happily-ever-afters are guaranteed—along with a little chaos, a lot of heart, and the kind of chemistry that makes your eReader blush.

Fast love. Fierce devotion. Delicious fantasies.

Violet is the original creator of the following multi author series':

Monster Between the Sheets

Dad Bod: Men Built for Comfort

Dad Bod: Large and in Charge

Dad Bod: Christmas

Dad Bod: Monster Edition

Filthy Fairy Tales